D1236687

— WILDERNESS RIDGE —

TROPHY BUCK

BY ART COULSON · ILLUSTRATED BY JOHANNA TARKELA

STONE ARCH BOOKS
a capstone imprint

Published by Stone Arch Books, an imprint of Capstone.
1710 Roe Crest Drive
North Mankato, Minnesota 56003
capstonepub.com

Library of Congress Cataloging-in-Publication Data
Names: Coulson, Art, 1961– author. | Tarkela, Johanna, illustrator.
Title: Trophy buck / by Art Coulson ; illustrated by Johanna Tarkela.
Description: North Mankato, Minnesota : Stone Arch Books, an imprint of Capstone, 2022. | Series: Wilderness ridge | Audience: Ages 8–11. | Audience: Grades 4–6. | Summary: Excited to go on his first family hunting trip, twelve-year-old Rodney learns Cherokee traditions, gun safety, and patience.
Identifiers: LCCN 2021002837 (print) | LCCN 2021002838 (ebook) | ISBN 9781663912275 (hardcover) | ISBN 9781663921956 (paperback) | ISBN 9781663912244 (ebook pdf)
Subjects: CYAC: Hunting—Fiction. | Cherokee Indians—Fiction. | Indians of North America—Oklahoma—Fiction.
Classification: LCC PZ7.1.C6758 Tr 2022 (print) | LCC PZ7.1.C6758 (ebook) | DDC [Fic]—dc23
LC record available at https://lccn.loc.gov/2021002837
LC ebook record available at https://lccn.loc.gov/2021002838

Editorial Credits
Editor: Alison Deering; Designer: Sarah Bennett; Media Researcher: Svetlana Zhurkin; Production Specialist: Katy LaVigne

Design elements: Shutterstock: Mikhail Zyablov, SvartKat

All internet sites appearing in back matter were available and accurate when this book was sent to press.

Printed and bound in the USA. 4270

Table of Contents

CHAPTER ONE

Anticipation

Why is everything I want to do such a pain?
I thought. *Can't a guy just have some fun?*

I had been dreaming of going hunting
with my family as far back as I could
remember. I was finally twelve—old enough
to go to my family's deer camp this fall—and
now my dad was insisting I had to go to some
sort of school first.

"It's hunter safety class, not boarding
school, Rodney," Dad said. "You'll survive.
Hunter safety courses make safer hunters.
They teach you important skills you'll need
out at the deer camp."

"Yeah, but it's all day! On a Saturday! Can't you and everyone else just teach me what I need to know once we get there?" I said.

My whole family hunted together every year. Well, at least the adults did. I would be hunting with my aunts, uncles, Dad, and my grandma.

My mom would be there this year too. Most years, she stayed home with me. But this year, she'd be coming along because I was finally old enough to hunt with my family.

But despite all that, I could tell from Dad's face the answer was still no.

"Hunter safety class will teach you about your responsibilities as a hunter," Dad said. "You'll learn about the parts of your gun, how to care for it, and, most importantly, how to handle it safely at all times. You need to know those things, Chooch."

The nickname was familiar but not unique to just my family. A lot of Cherokee kids were called *chooch* or *choogie*, short for *ah-joo-ja*—"boy" in the Cherokee language.

"I know, Dad, but—"

"But nothing, Rodney," Dad stopped me. "You'll learn about game animals and their habitats. And why we do everything we can to respect and protect those places. You'll learn to identify different types of animals in the wild. And the instructor will show you how to dress a deer in the field. There's just so much to learn."

"Yeah, and I could learn it from you," I argued.

Dad shook his head. "Your aunts and uncles and I can teach you a lot, but it's best to learn the basics first. You'll get to camp with the knowledge you need to begin the hunt safely."

He gave me a firm look. "I took the hunter safety course when I was your age. So did your grandpa. It's what you do."

I sighed. There was no point in arguing.

Dad walked back toward the den. "And speaking of your grandfather, I know there's something he would have wanted you to have."

I perked up. I had to admit, I was a little curious. Okay, okay, a lot curious.

"You're going to need a gun to use for your first hunt," Dad said, returning to the room.

In his hands was the most beautiful rifle I had ever seen.

"It's a Remington model 700," Dad said as he handed the gun to me. "This was my first gun. Your grandpa gave it to me when I was just about your age. And you know what? I got my first deer with this rifle. Just like Grandpa did."

I turned the rifle over in my hands, inspecting every square inch of wood and metal. It was a bolt-action rifle, just like the one Dad and I shot at the Rod and Gun Club range a few times a year.

The wooden grip and forestock had a carved diamond pattern. It was a little worn but still beautiful. The blued-steel barrel smelled of gun oil and tangy metal.

I worked the smooth bolt action. Then I pulled the stock to my shoulder and peered down the barrel.

"Careful there," Dad said, putting his hand on my arm. "Never aim a gun at something you don't intend to shoot. And never aim at another person, even if you're sure the gun isn't loaded. Safety first. Safety always."

I lowered the rifle and continued to inspect it.

"You'll learn all about safe gun handling tomorrow in the hunter safety course," Dad added.

I sighed. I was going to hunter safety class, whether I wanted to or not.

CHAPTER TWO

Hunter Safety

The next morning, we drove down to Wagoner for my all-day school. And just like a school day, there was no sleeping in. Dad woke me up at what felt like the crack of dawn.

"Come on, Rodney, rise and shine!" Dad said, throwing open my bedroom door.

I grumbled, but Dad was having none of it. He yanked the comforter off me before leaving my room.

I dragged myself out of bed and into the shower. Thirty minutes later, we were pulling into the civic center parking lot.

Dad handed me a bag lunch before I got out of the car. "It'll be fun," he said. "Really. Plus, you'll be one big step closer to going to deer camp."

I sighed. At least he had a point there.

I walked into the building and followed the signs to the assigned classroom. I was surprised to see that the students weren't just kids my age. There were some grown-ups there too.

An older man took his place at the front of the room. "My name is Mr. Buzzard," he introduced himself. "I'm sure you're all eager to learn about hunter safety, so let's get started."

He got right into the lessons. The beginning was a little boring. He mostly talked about why the course was important, our responsibility as hunters, and how the state managed all of the wildlife areas—all the info my dad had already told me.

He also went over some basic hunter safety info, writing each rule on the whiteboard and explaining as he went.

- Assume that every gun is loaded, even if you just unloaded it.

- Control the direction of the muzzle— always point the gun in a safe direction. Never aim at anything you don't intend to shoot.

- Keep your finger off the trigger until ready to fire.

- Be certain of your target and of what's behind it.

- When hunting for deer and other large game, you must wear a hunter orange hat and outer garment so you can be seen by other hunters.

It felt like it took *forever*, but finally Mr. Buzzard got to the good stuff—rifles and shotguns.

First, he showed us several real weapons. Then, he pointed out the different parts of the guns and told us how they worked.

"Besides being safe, the most important thing to remember when hunting is to take your time when shooting," Mr. Buzzard said. "Breathe slowly. Look down your barrel or through your scope and aim carefully. Then squeeze the trigger very slowly. Never jerk or pull it."

Dad had told me the same thing when we shot his rifle at the range. Everything had to be done slowly. A hunter had to be patient.

A kid in the back of the room raised his hand. Mr. Buzzard stopped talking and called on him. "Yes?"

"Do we get to shoot these guns today?" the kid asked.

I looked at Mr. Buzzard anxiously. I really hoped the answer was yes.

"Not today," Mr. Buzzard said. "There's another course you can sign up for after this one that includes shooting guns at the range. But today's class is strictly classroom lessons."

I looked back at the kid and shrugged my shoulders. He looked as disappointed as I felt. But then I remembered the Remington my dad had given me. It was way better than any of these guns. I couldn't wait to use it to get a trophy buck!

The class went on all day, but I was surprised at how much I liked it. Mr. Buzzard even showed us his field kit. He unzipped a small black bag that held a hunting knife and sharpening stone, a folding shovel, some rope, and a couple of cloth bags with holes in them.

After that, we watched a video on how to field dress a deer. I could see several kids squirming in their seats as the video played. But I knew field dressing was an important part of hunting.

Then came the worst part of the day—a pop quiz. Ugh. Just like school. But I got one-hundred percent.

I really felt like I was ready. My first hunt was just around the corner.

CHAPTER THREE

Opening Day at Last!

The next few weeks seemed to drag by. I cleaned my gun—five times. I studied the hunting websites for the state of Oklahoma and the Cherokee Nation. When my deer permit and Dad's license came in the mail from the Cherokee Nation, I thought I would explode from excitement.

Somehow, I managed to stay in one piece.

My parents even tortured me by taking me out to the deer camp for a day—but not to hunt. We spent the whole time cleaning and getting the cabin ready.

My uncles mowed grass and chopped wood. My aunts made beds and checked on the tree stands. Mom and her brother, Uncle Angus, checked on the pots and pans and other kitchen stuff. Boring.

The only good part was helping my dad set up our pop-up deer blind, where we'd be hunting, in his lucky spot.

I was starting to feel like I'd never actually get to hunt. Then, *finally*, the big day arrived. I didn't think I'd be able to stand it as we drove from our house to the camp an hour away.

Mom parked our car near the others. I practically jumped out while it was still moving. I grabbed my backpack and my rifle from the back and ran toward the cabin.

"Not so fast, Chooch!" Grandma yelled.

I stopped dead in my tracks. I knew better than to ignore my grandma. Everyone did.

Grandma could hug you and love you one minute. But she'd grab you fast as a snake if you misbehaved.

"Did you need me for something, Elisi?" I asked her, using the Cherokee word for "Grandma."

"Don't you be running off. Help unload the cars, and let's get this camp settled," she said. "We have a lot to do before sunup tomorrow. And you're going to want to eat tonight. Those coolers won't carry themselves into the kitchen."

I sighed. More work to do. I just wanted to hunt!

Even before we finished unloading all of the guns and gear, I could smell something good coming from the kitchen. Uncle Angus and Mom had started whipping up a big pot of spaghetti. From the smell of it, they were toasting garlic bread too.

Uncle Angus was a professional chef. He worked at a fancy restaurant in Tulsa. My family always ate the best food when he was around. I'd say he was probably the most popular person at deer camp.

"Mmmmm, mmm. Uganasda! That smells deee-licious," Uncle Archie said as he dropped a heavy duffle bag on the porch. "Where do you want all this stuff, Edna?"

"Just throw it on one of the bunks," said Aunt Edna. "We can sleep in the same beds as last year."

After dinner, we carried folding chairs out to the firepit. My dad had a roaring bonfire already lit. The sun was going down, and the trees all around us were darkening from gray to black.

Uncle Archie started to strum his guitar. Uncle Cyrus pulled a harmonica out of his pocket.

As they played, Uncle Angus started to sing a song in the Cherokee language. Grandma joined in. Their voices sounded beautiful together.

Whenever my family got together, you could count on two things. One, we'd eat a ton of food. Two, there would be a Cherokee gospel sing by the fire.

Grandma and Uncle Angus sang a song called "One Drop of Blood." Grandma had told me our relatives brought the song with them on the Trail of Tears. That's when the Cherokee people had walked from their homes in the Old Country—Tennessee, Georgia, and North Carolina—all the way to Oklahoma.

Soldiers had forced our people to leave their lands. They'd had to walk through the cold and snow to a new place called Indian Territory. A lot of Cherokee people had died on the trail.

Grandma had told me we must never forget. "These songs are one way to remember," she'd said.

I walked over to where Grandma was sitting and hugged her. Then I went over to Uncle Angus, who was holding out a s'more.

"Gourmet s'mores, Chooch," he said with a wink. "I bet they would charge you fifty, sixty dollars for one of these in my restaurant. Serve it on a china plate and everything."

I went back to my chair to enjoy my treat. I felt all warm inside. I'm not sure why. It was plenty cold out. But the fire was nice. And listening to my family sing together and speak the Cherokee language made me feel like I belonged to something bigger than me. Bigger than my family even.

Pretty soon, my mom walked over and put her hand on my shoulder.

"Time for bed, little man," she said. "Dawn is going to come awfully early."

I didn't even remember getting undressed and into bed. But that night, I dreamt of hunting. I saw a big buck. He walked right up to me and said, "Don't forget to say the right words."

CHAPTER FOUR

Hunting, Finally

Before it was even light out, I smelled coffee brewing. Someone was shaking my shoulder.

"Wake up, Rodney," Dad said. "Come on. We have to start the hunt the right way."

Everyone else was already up. The adults all grabbed their coffee mugs and headed out the front door into the darkness. Everyone was wearing jackets, hats, and gloves—all bright orange so it would be easy for the other hunters to see them out in the field.

I followed Dad and Mom down the hill from camp to the creek. My relatives started to wash themselves in the cold water.

"What's going on?" I asked Dad in a whisper. "Aren't we supposed to be going hunting?"

"Yes," Dad said. "But we Cherokee people have certain hunting traditions and ceremonies that many of our elders still follow. We always start deer camp by going to water and having one of the elders say a prayer."

Mom pointed to me and to the water. I leaned down and tried to do what everyone else was doing. First I washed my face. Then I splashed more cold water on my forehead and chest.

Uncle Archie stood up and looked at everyone. Then he started to speak in Cherokee. It sounded like a prayer.

I could only understand a word or two of what he was saying. But I knew *Unetlanvhi* meant "the creator."

Finally we walked back up the hill to our camp. The ceremony had only taken a few minutes, but I was anxious to head to our blind and start hunting. Even so, I was glad to have started the day the right way with my family.

"Grab your gun and don't forget your hat and gloves," Dad said. "It's cold out."

He was right about that. My feet were already starting to chill in my boots.

Dad hung his rifle over his shoulder, then grabbed a thermos of coffee and a folding camp chair.

"Let's go. It's almost lunchtime already," he joked.

We wished everyone good luck and said goodbye to Mom. Then we were off.

"It's important to know where everyone else will be hunting this morning," Dad said as we walked. "Safety first. Safety always."

"Everyone has a favorite hunting spot," Dad told me. "Uncle Angus and Uncle Cyrus like their tree stands down by a group of pawpaw trees. Uncle Archie and Aunt Edna usually hunt on foot, away from everyone else."

"Why?" I asked.

"Grandma says they mostly just like to hike in the woods together," Dad said with a laugh. "They don't really care if they get any deer."

"What about Grandma?" I asked.

"She has a tree stand back closer to the cabin," he replied. "Your grandma doesn't like to have to walk too far when it's time for lunch or to use the restroom."

Dad walked quickly through the fields toward the pop-up deer blind we'd set up on our earlier visit. The dark camo blind sat just inside the tree line at the edge of a clearing. It had a large, diamond-shaped orange piece of cloth attached to the front for safety.

Dad set up his chair near the window facing the clearing. He closed the door by fastening the hooks and loops.

"Time to learn the meaning of patience, son," he said. "We might sit here all day and not see a deer. But we have to stay quiet and try not to move too much."

I nodded. The inside of the blind was small. I was excited about hunting but not about standing inside the cramped space. Our chairs, Dad's field kit, and my pack took up most of the floor space. My legs felt like they might tighten up and cramp, and we had only been in the blind for a few minutes.

"Keep an eye out the window toward the field, Rodney. You should see some deer wander by eventually," Dad said. "But tell me if you get tired. You can sit down, and I'll keep watch."

No way was I going to get tired. I was way too excited for that, leg cramps or no leg cramps.

Dad showed me how to chamber a round and made sure my safety was on. "If you wait to chamber the round until you see a deer, the deer will hear it and run," he explained in a whisper.

Then Dad looked at me kind of weird. It was like he was somewhere else, looking at something I couldn't see.

"I was standing just about where you are on my first hunt with your grandpa," he whispered. "A large buck walked right into that clearing over there." He tilted his head toward the field.

"It was my first deer," he said. "I used that rifle. It helped to feed our family all winter. I don't think your grandpa was ever more proud of me."

I hoped I would have that chance today. I couldn't wait to see a big buck walk into the field.

I'd carefully take aim with my new rifle. I would drop the buck with one shot, then use the lessons from my hunter safety course when I field dressed him. It would be the best day of my life.

Just then . . . *crack!* A branch snapped as something large walked toward us.

CHAPTER FIVE

Trophy Buck

Dad and I both startled. He put his finger to his lips and motioned for me to stay very still.

Crack!

The footsteps were getting nearer.

Crack!

Every loud noise made me jump a little. I could feel my heart thumping in my chest. My head was tingling under my hat.

I scanned the field and the tree line to both sides. Was this a big buck? Would this be my first deer?

Then I saw him.

The buck had a large rack of antlers with points spreading out in all directions. It had to be at least a ten- or twelve-point buck. A trophy buck.

The buck stepped out of the woods about thirty yards to our left. He stopped and snorted. His ears twitched. He slowly turned his head and snorted again. Then he twitched his white tail and took another step.

I quickly raised my gun to my shoulder. This was it. I looked down the barrel and sighted in on the buck's right shoulder.

Dad put his hand on my arm and shook his head. "Slowly. Slowly, Rodney," he whispered. "Take your time. Breathe. Flick off the safety. Aim carefully. Put your finger on the trigger. Don't pull it— squeeze. Squeeeeeze."

"I know, Dad. I know," I whispered back impatiently.

I turned back toward the field and raised my gun to my eye again, but I was too excited to take my time. I jerked the trigger and fired. *Boom!*

The recoil pushed me back a bit. I lost sight of the deer for a moment.

I refocused and realized, *Oh, no! I missed him!*

The buck ran off. I watched as it leapt across the field and into the woods on the other side.

It all happened so quickly that I didn't even have time to chamber another round. There was no chance for me to take a second shot.

I felt like crying. I had done everything wrong. I'd done all the things my dad had warned me not to.

I had rushed the shot. I'd jerked the trigger instead of gently squeezing it. And I hadn't taken enough time to aim before taking my shot.

"It's okay, son. You'll get another chance," Dad said. He put his arm around my shoulder and squeezed me. I could tell he was trying to make me feel better. "Did you learn anything?"

I nodded, and my eyes watered. "I was impatient," I said, staring down at my feet. "I went too fast."

"But you learned something. And you won't make that mistake again. That's what's important," Dad said. "Every hunt teaches us something."

He picked up his thermos and his rifle. "Let's break for the morning," he suggested. "We can go see what Angus has whipped up for lunch."

I nodded and followed Dad back to the cabin. But the whole way I couldn't stop thinking one thing. I still had a lot to learn about hunting.

CHAPTER SIX

Second Chance

Uncle Angus, with some help from Mom and Aunt Edna, had outdone himself. He had set up a hog fry outside the cabin on a portable gas burner. Mom made her famous brown beans and greens. Aunt Edna whipped up several skillets full of sweet corn bread.

I ate quietly while everyone else talked and laughed. The delicious food almost made me forget the terrible morning I'd had and my missed shot at a trophy buck. Almost.

"Instead of going back to the blind, what do you say we hunt on foot this afternoon?" Dad asked me between bites of corn bread.

I shrugged.

"We could walk the edge of the woods," Dad continued. "Away from where everyone else is hunting, and look for deer. Might have more luck than just sitting in one place all afternoon."

"Okay," I said. I looked back down at my plate.

"You'll get another chance, son," Dad said. "Don't be discouraged."

After we helped to clean up from lunch, we put our orange coats and hats back on, grabbed our guns, and headed back outside. Dad made sure everyone else knew what our plan was and where we intended to hunt this afternoon.

It had warmed up a bit, but the air still smelled like fall. We walked down the hill toward the stream where we had started the day.

Before we crossed, Dad stopped. "Make sure your gun is unloaded," he said.

"Why?" I asked.

"In case you fall. You don't want your gun to go off and hurt you or someone else," he said. "Always make sure your gun is unloaded before you cross a stream, climb over a fence, or climb up into a tree stand. Safety first. Safety always."

After we crossed the stream, we paused to reload our rifles. Then we hiked along the edge of the woods. We stopped every now and then to scan the field to our left and to listen.

"You know, Rodney, sometimes you can hunt every day during the season and never get a deer," Dad said. "One year, when you were about four or five, I came to camp with your grandma, grandpa, and uncles. Not one of us got a deer."

"I bet you guys were so disappointed,"
I said. "What a waste. No one got a trophy
buck."

Dad shrugged. "We were disappointed,
sure. But we enjoyed being out here, hunting
our land and carrying on a tradition that
goes back hundreds of years. Maybe longer."

I thought about that for a minute. I was
enjoying my time with Dad and the rest of
my family. I was learning a lot.

*Maybe getting a big buck isn't the only thing
that makes a good hunter,* I thought.

I was just about to say so when Dad held
up his hand. I turned to see what he was
looking at.

Across the meadow stood a young buck.
It had a six-point rack and was much smaller
than the trophy buck I missed this morning.
It was still a beauty.

Dad looked at me and nodded.

I carefully brought my rifle around and worked the bolt action as quietly as I could. Then I took a deep breath and slowly raised the rifle to my eyes.

CHAPTER SEVEN

Not Again

Time seemed to slow down. Every breath I took lasted a lifetime.

I blinked and pulled the rifle snug against my shoulder. I let out a long, silent breath. Then I thumbed the safety and sighted down the barrel, lining up my shot.

My heart was beating in my throat as I focused on the buck. I could feel my shoulders tense up. Sweat dripped down my forehead and into my eyes. It took all of my willpower not to reach up with my sleeve and wipe my eyes.

The buck stood about seventy-five yards from us, far enough away that he hadn't heard me work the bolt action. Thankfully, the light breeze was coming toward us, so he hadn't smelled us either.

The animal flicked his ears but didn't seem nervous or afraid. He reached his head down to eat some tall grass at the edge of the field.

Another breath.

"Take your time," Dad whispered. "Steady."

I squeezed the trigger gently, smoothly, slowly. I was determined not to make the same mistake I'd made last time.

But in the split second before my shot went off, the deer sensed danger. He raised his head, flipped his white tail, and ran off.

I could feel my whole body slump.

"Oh, man," Dad said. "That was a tough one."

"What did I do wrong?" I asked.

Dad shook his head. "You couldn't have done anything differently. Your technique was perfect. Sometimes deer just get spooked. It's like they have some sort of sixth sense."

I flipped my safety back on, sat down on the ground, and laid my rifle across my lap. I put my head in my hands and closed my eyes tight.

"These things happen, Rodney. A hunter needs to learn patience," Dad said. "It's why we call it hunting and not eating."

I looked up at Dad. He was actually grinning. Grinning!

"Not helping, Dad," I said. "I'm really frustrated. Can you not make it into a joke?"

Dad immediately stopped smiling. "You're right," he said. "I'm sorry. I know this must be hard for you."

I nodded.

"But I promise you we'll keep trying," he said, helping me to my feet. "And you'll get your deer one day soon."

Dad gathered up his gear and looked back toward camp.

"Let's call it a day," he said. "Tomorrow is another day. Your luck is bound to change. And besides, I hear Uncle Angus is whipping up some of his world-famous venison chili and fry bread for dinner tonight. It's one of my favorite meals every year."

"Yum," I said. At least I'd have a good meal to look forward to.

Dad stopped and looked at me over his shoulder. He winked. "Just don't be alarmed if you hear weird noises coming from your uncles' bunks after everyone is asleep," he said. "We love Angus's chili. But it doesn't always love us back."

CHAPTER EIGHT

Back to the Blind

I heard Grandma talking with Uncle Archie and Uncle Cyrus before I was really awake the next morning. They were speaking softly in the Cherokee language and laughing.

I smelled coffee and bacon. My stomach growled loudly.

"What's that, Rodney?" Uncle Angus asked as he cracked eggs into a bowl. Everyone laughed.

"Tsayosihas?" Grandma asked me. "You hungry?"

"Vv. Agiyosihv," I said as I dropped from the top bunk to the floor. "I'm always hungry."

That made everyone laugh again. Grandma smiled. I could tell she was proud that I'd answered her in our Cherokee language.

Everyone gathered around the big table.

"Rodney and I will be hunting in our blind again this morning," Dad told the group as we ate.

My heart started thumping. Maybe I would have another chance at that big buck. And this time I would remember everything I'd learned. *Take my time. Aim carefully. Slowly squeeze the trigger.* That would help me get my trophy buck.

After breakfast Dad and I walked up the trail along the edge of the woods. Dad put a hand on my shoulder and pulled me closer to him. He didn't say anything. He didn't really have to. I knew he loved me and was happy to be hunting with me.

We set up in the blind just like yesterday. I chambered a round and made sure my safety was on. Then we waited and watched. Then we waited some more.

As the sun came up, it started to get a little warm in the blind. My eyes started to get heavy.

"Rodney, you need to stay alert," Dad whispered. "Never forget you have a loaded weapon in your hands. If you need to rest your eyes, let's unload your rifle and you can have a seat."

"No, it's okay. I'm awake," I said. I did *not* want to miss my chance to get that buck.

A few minutes later, Dad straightened and put his finger to his lips. He nodded toward the clearing. A pair of does wandered out of the woods and began to eat.

"Let's wait a minute and see if your buck is with them," Dad whispered.

But the two does walked along by themselves. Soon, one of them turned back and headed into the woods. The other stayed in the clearing.

"I know it's not your buck, but she's yours if you want the shot," Dad said.

I nodded, raised my gun, and thumbed off the safety. I slowly exhaled and took aim. I squeezed the trigger.

The deer fell before the sound of my shot faded. My first deer!

"Way to go, Chooch!" Dad said. "I'm proud of you. Nice work!"

We set down our guns, and Dad grabbed his field bag. We walked over to the deer. Dad knelt down and put two fingers to the animal's neck.

"I'm feeling for a pulse," he explained. Then he looked down at the deer and spoke softly in Cherokee.

I raised an eyebrow. "What are you doing?"

"I was asking for the deer's forgiveness," Dad said. "I told her that we would be respectful with her and that she would help us feed our family. We have to remember to say the right words when we take an animal's life."

Say the right words, I thought. Just like the buck had said in my dream the first night. Now that was weird.

Dad pulled a hunting knife and rubber gloves out of his bag. He handed me a pair of the blue gloves.

"Put these on," he said. "Time to practice what you learned in your hunter safety class."

After we dressed the doe, Dad went into the woods and came back with a big branch. He tied the doe's hooves to the branch so we could hoist the branch onto our shoulders and carry her back to camp.

It was hard work carrying the doe and our gear, but I didn't mind. I had never been more excited to do some work in my life. My first deer!

CHAPTER NINE

Family Celebration

The campfire had burned down to hot coals, and Uncle Angus glistened with sweat as he stirred the big cast-iron stew pot.

My stomach growled. The smells drifting toward me—venison stew made with my first deer—were unbelievable.

"First bowl goes to the successful hunter," Uncle Angus said, handing me a bowl of stew.

I smiled and looked down at the steaming bowl. Then I walked over to my grandma.

"Here, Elisi," I said, holding out the bowl. "Elders first. This stew is for you. And it's made with the deer I got today."

Grandma smiled. She looked at me and nodded her head.

"Wado, Chooch. Uganasda," she said, blowing on a chunk of venison before taking a bite. "Thank you. It's delicious."

After we had all eaten our fill of stew and corn bread, I helped Mom and Grandma carry in the plates and silverware. I could hear everyone talking and laughing around the fire.

When we got back outside, Uncle Archie was just finishing telling a story about a weird one-antlered buck. Apparently he and Aunt Edna had seen it while hunting this afternoon.

"Did you shoot it?" I asked.

Everyone stopped laughing and looked at me.

"What?" I said. I had no idea what everyone was looking at.

"That's bad luck," Aunt Edna answered. "You let those ones go. We watched that one-horn go on his way, then Archie had to say a little prayer before we could start hunting again."

I nodded. There were a lot of the old ways I didn't know yet. But I was learning.

"Hey, tell us about the deer we just ate," Uncle Cyrus said. "Your first deer. You're now a provider for our family. We're grateful that you shared your meat with us."

I sat up taller in my chair. "Well, it wasn't easy," I said. "Before I got my doe, Dad and I put in a lot of hard work. I missed two nice bucks yesterday."

I paused and looked over at Dad. "But I guess that's why we call it hunting and not eating."

My whole family laughed. Dad winked at me.

I had to put in a lot of work before my first hunt. I'd even gone to school on a Saturday! But it had been worth it. I'd gotten my first deer! Sure, I hadn't bagged my trophy buck. But I knew I'd be back next year. And I'd remember everything I'd learned.

About the Author

photo by Ivy Vainio

Art Coulson, Cherokee, was an award-winning journalist and the first executive director of the Wilma Mankiller Foundation in Oklahoma. He grew up hunting for squirrels, rabbits, and deer with his father, brother, grandfather, aunts, and uncles. His first children's book, *The Creator's Game: A Story of Baaga'adowe/Lacrosse* (Minnesota Historical Society Press, 2013), told of the deep spiritual and cultural connections of American Indian people to the sport of lacrosse. Art still plays traditional Cherokee stickball, an original version of lacrosse, when he is visiting friends and family in the Cherokee Nation of Oklahoma. Art lives in Apple Valley, Minnesota.

About the Illustrator

photo by Johanna Tarkela

Johanna Tarkela is a digital artist who loves playing with strong, atmospheric light and shadow in her realistic-style work. Born and raised in Finland, she spent a lot of her childhood outdoors and surrounded by the beautiful Nordic nature, which reflects in her favorite themes to draw. She has been drawing since she was a young child and has worked on many children's books. Johanna later attended university to study illustration in England, where she currently resides and works as a freelance illustrator, represented by Lemonade Illustration Agency.

Glossary

blind (BLYND)—a hidden place from which hunters can shoot deer

buck (BUHK)—a male deer older than one year

doe (DOH)—a female deer older than one year

field dressing (FEELD DRES-ing)—the process of removing the organs of hunted game; a necessary step in preserving meat from animals harvested in the wild

forestock (FOR-stahk)—the gun part located underneath the back end of the barrel

game (geym)—animals hunted for sport or for food

habitat (HAB-uh-tat)—the natural place and conditions in which an animal lives

license (LYE-suhnss)—a document that gives official permission to do something

muzzle (MUHZ-uhl)—the discharging end of a weapon

permit (PUR-mit)—a written statement giving permission for something

recoil (RI-koil)—the kickback of a gun when firing

round (ROUND)—a single bullet fired by a gun

safety (SAYF-tee)—a device that prevents a gun from firing

scope (skohp)—an instrument on a gun used for viewing

technique (tek-NEEK)—a method or a way of doing something that requires skill

venison (VEN-uh-suhn)—the meat of a deer

Talk About It

1. The Locust family has many special traditions that they follow at their hunting camp. Look back through the story and identify some of them. Why do you think those traditions are important?

2. Rodney is not excited to go to hunter safety class. He thinks he can learn everything he needs from his family. Do you think hunter safety classes are important? Why or why not? Talk about your reasoning.

3. The night before his first hunt, Rodney dreams of a buck telling him, "Don't forget to say the right words." What do you think that dream meant? Have you ever had a dream that later came true? Talk about it.

Write About It

1. Rodney is sure he knows what he's doing, but his overconfidence costs him a trophy buck. Write a paragraph about a time you learned a valuable lesson after making a mistake or failing when you tried to do something.

2. What are some of the dos and don'ts a hunter must keep in mind when hunting for deer? Write a list of tips you learned from this story.

3. Have you ever been on a hunt yourself? Write about one of your favorite hunting memories. (If you haven't been, imagine the perfect hunt.) What made (or would make) that hunt memorable?

More About Deer Hunting

People have been hunting deer for thousands of years. In the United States, more than eleven million people hunt deer each year. Venison, or deer meat, is a healthy food and has long been an important part of the diet of Native American people.

There are many different types of deer around the world that are hunted for their meat. The two main types of deer hunted in the United States are mule deer, found mostly in the West, and whitetail deer, found east of the Rocky Mountains.

Male deer, called bucks, grow a set of antlers each summer and lose their racks during the winter. When the antlers first grow, they are covered with velvet. The velvet falls off as the antlers begin to harden in the fall. Bucks will often rub off the velvet by scraping their antlers against trees. Female deer, called does, give birth to one to three fawns in the spring. Fawns stay with their mothers for one to two years.

Deer hunting is controlled by states and tribal governments. They set seasons for different types of hunting, such as rifle and shotgun, archery, and muzzle loaders. Some states and tribes hold special hunts for youth or to allow hunters to harvest only antlerless deer. Some tribes restrict hunting to tribal citizens only.

Deer seasons vary by state and tribe but mostly take place in the summer or fall. In Oklahoma and the Cherokee Nation, where this story takes place, gun deer season runs from late November to early December.

In some states and tribal nations, including Oklahoma and the Cherokee Nation, new hunters must take a hunter safety course. In others, wildlife officials strongly encourage but do not require hunter safety courses. For a list of courses, visit the U.S. Fish and Wildlife Service's website (fws.gov), or look up the natural resources department for your state or tribe.

Check Out All the Wilderness Ridge Titles

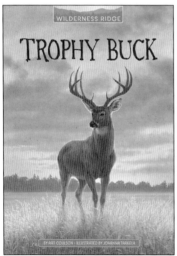